JUL 1 8 2021

D0371634

TBH, No One Can
EVER Know

Also by Lisa Greenwald

The Friendship List Series
11 Before 12
12 Before 13
13 and Counting
13 and 3/4

The TBH Series
TBH, This Is SO Awkward
TBH, This May Be TMI
TBH, Too Much Drama
TBH, IDK What's Next
TBH, I Feel the Same
TBH, You Know What I Mean

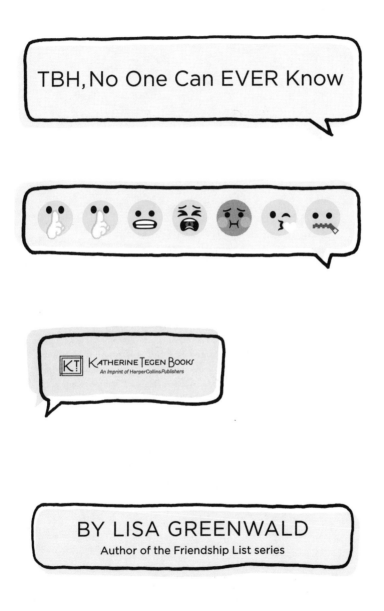

TBH, No One Can EVER Know

KATHERINE TEGEN BOOKS
An Imprint of HarperCollins Publishers

BY LISA GREENWALD
Author of the Friendship List series

Katherine Tegen Books is an imprint of HarperCollins Publishers.

TBH, No One Can EVER Know
Copyright © 2021 by Lisa Greenwald
Emoji icons provided by EmojiOne
All rights reserved. Printed in the United States of America.
No part of this book may be used or reproduced in any manner whatsoever without written permission except in the case of brief quotations embodied in critical articles and reviews. For information address HarperCollins Children's Books, a division of HarperCollins Publishers, 195 Broadway, New York, NY 10007.
www.harpercollinschildrens.com

ISBN 978-0-06-299181-2

Typography by Molly Fehr
20 21 22 23 24   PC/LSCC   10 9 8 7 6 5 4 3 2 1
First Edition

For all of the readers

YORKVILLE MIDDLE SCHOOL

Yorkville Middle School Text Alert: Today is a SNOW DAY! All Yorkville schools are closed, and after-school activities and meetings are canceled. Stay warm & dry!

FRIENDSSSSSSSS

V C G P

VICTORIA

OMGGGGGGGGG 😦 😦 😦

SNOW DAYYYYYYYYYY ☃

CECILY

Woo 🐧 👏 🐧 👏

GABRIELLE

Soooooo happy 😛 😛 😆 😄 🥳

NO MATH TEST FOR ME ✖ ➕ ➖ ➗

PRIANKA

Guysssss 😒 😒 😔 😳

I went back to bed & u all just woke me up
😴 😫 😫 💤 🛏

Blarrrggghhhhhhh 😴 😴 😴 😴 😴 😴

VICTORIA

Sorry, Pri 😒 😒

GABRIELLE

Can we all go sledding @ the golf course
later? ⛄ ❄ ⛄

VICTORIA

Oooh yeah! 👏 👏

2

VICTORIA

Will beg my mom to let me go

PRIANKA

LOL, Vic

What is she scared of

It's sledding not bungee jumping 💡

VICTORIA

Ugghhhhh I don't even know 😖 😖 😖

CECILY

I'll see about sledding

May stay cozy @ 🏠

VICTORIA

Blargh, Cece

CECILY

Gonna go make breakfast 🤚 🤚

Ttyl 😙 😙

3

Gabrielle, Mom

G   M

MOM

Gabs?

Are you up?

GABRIELLE

Yes

Hi

MOM

Mrs. Minkin is worried about slipping on the snow when she has to take Elroy out. Can you help her take him out?

GABRIELLE

Ok

Give me 10 min

Don't want to get up 😴 😴 😴 😴

MOM

I think he has to pee

Come now, please

Will be a mitzvah

GABRIELLE

Ok

Coming

MOM

Love you

Dear Diary,

Hi, it's me, Cecily. I think I should come up with a
better name for you since you're brand-new. Thank
you, Ingrid, for this fab Christmas gift. Don't know
why I'm thanking her here since she can't see this (AT

LEAST I HOPE SHE WON'T SEE THIS!) but anyway.

So, hmmm. Where to start? Well, the thing is, I still have feelings for Mara. Sometimes they go away or maybe they're just in the back of my mind when I'm busy but then when I see her for a long span of time or talk to her, I feel like I like her again.

She just looks at me in a different way than anyone else. And I can't explain it; I just want to be near her. I mean, I know I bailed on the summer trip with her, and I felt bad about it but it was the right decision. But now I like her all over again.

UGGG!!!

I never want to text first because I hate waiting around for her to text back. It stresses me out waiting for those three dots that show she's typing.

This is a depressing way to start you, my new beautiful journal, but what can I do?

Here's some happy news, though: TODAY IS A SNOW DAY! SO WOO! Maybe she'll come sledding . . .

Xoxoxo Cecily

Ivy, Gabrielle

IVY

Gabs! Do you have a snow day today? ❄️ ❄️

GABRIELLE

YES! You? ⛄ 🎉 ⛄

IVY

Yesssssssssss 🐧 🐧

I miss you soooooooo much 😪 🐱

I wish we lived closer 🐱

How many more days until summerrrrrrr camp ☀️ 🌞 ☀️ 😎

GABRIELLE

Ha too many 🐱

IVY

How are you my love

GABRIELLE

Eh

I'm ok

IVY

Just ok?

GABRIELLE

Well school is still sooooo hard 😴 😴 😴 😴

I just don't feel like I have "my thing."

Ya know?

IVY

Ummmmm 🤔 🤔 🤔

No idea what u mean

For real

GABRIELLE

Ha ok. Like, everyone has something they're passionate about. And I don't have that. I don't have my one thing that I'm really good at

IVY

Oh yeah

Hmmmmm 🤫 🤫 🤫

Well you gotta explore your passions 🩶 🩶

GABRIELLE

I know

Duh LOL 😆 🤣 😆 😝

What's your passion? 🤫

IVY

Ummmm learning about other countries I think

9

Hmmmm. See! That's cool

I'll help u find your thing 🐧🐧✨✨✨✨✨✨

K thanx

Gotta go 👋👋😘

Going sledding

K have fun 😘 😘

FRIENDSSSSSSSS

V   C   G   P

GABRIELLE

On my way 4 sledding! 🛷 ⛄ ❄️ 🌥️ ⛄

CECILY

Same!

PRIANKA

Me too 🌷❗🌷❗

So glad you're joining, Cece! 🎿 🎿 🎿 🎿

VICTORIA

Yaaaayyyyyyy 👏 👏

I had to FOR REAL beg my mom
to let me go sledding

Like the most begging ever

SOOOO ANNOYING 😒 😒 😒

VICTORIA

Anyway whatever

Bundle up! 😬   ⛄

From: National Teen Poetry Competition
To: Prianka Basak
Subject: Congratulations!

Dear Ms. Basak:

We are pleased to share that your poem, "Follow the Wind," is the third-place winner in this year's National Teen Poetry Competition, sponsored by ***Poets Magazine***. More information will follow shortly about the awards ceremony.
Best wishes & congratulations!

Samuel F. Kingsley
National Teen Poetry Competition, Chairman

Prianka, Sage

P S

SAGE

Did u get the email

PRIANKA

Yesssssssss

SAGE

I'm so sad 😖 😧 🙁 🥺

PRIANKA

Oh no !!!!

SAGE

They thanked me for entering but I didn't win 😞 😞 🙁

Not even like 8th place 🙁

Did you

PRIANKA

Ummmm

SAGE

???

PRIANKA

I actually came in 3rd place 😊

SAGE

Wow

Congrats

PRIANKA

Are you sledding today ?

SAGE

No

I gotta go

PRIANKA

Xoxoxo 😘 😘 😘 😘

Gabrielle, Mom

MOM

Hi, Gabs. Hope you're having fun sledding. Please be careful! Also, Elroy needs a walk again when you get home. Thanks for helping out. Love you.

GABRIELLE

K, Mom, but why can't you take Elroy out? 🐶🐶😤😤😤

MOM

Gabrielle. Don't be rude.

Chocolate +
graham cracker +
marshmallow = perfect snow
day treat to remind you of
summer. Love, Cece

♡

FRIENDSSSSSSSS

V C G P

VICTORIA

Guys, has anyone seen Colin & Jared?

Their friends say they're missing

Every time we go down the hill
we get all spread out

Where is everyone

Totally freaking out

Victoria, Mom

V M

MOM

You left your laptop on

I can see your texts on your computer

Concerned about kids missing

Are you ok?

Were the kids found

Are you ok?

Victoria, hello?

Answer me now

Missed call from: Mom
Missed call from: Mom
Missed call from: Mom

Mom. Stop.

Just because my computer is open does not mean you need to snoop

Calm down

I'm fine.

FRIENDSSSSSSSS

V   C   G   P

GABRIELLE

Sorry just saw this

I know u sent forever ago

They were found 💯

Went to ice skate in boots on lake

GABRIELLE

Dummies 😒 😒 😒

Now videoing people going down the hill

So lame

And my mom keeps calling me to check in

Where r u guys now ❓❓

FRIENDSSSSSSSS

V C G P

CECILY

Hiiiii 👋 👋

Who wants to meet me @ top of hill for
one last run

Then walk

PRIANKA

Coming 🙍

Was with Vishal

I love him again BTW 😩 😩

GABRIELLE

LOL 😆 😆

Hi

Where is Vic now

VICTORIA

Hi

I'm home 😟 😟

My mom picked me up 😫 😳 😧 🙀

GABRIELLE

Omg why 😫 😫 😖 😣 😕 😕

VICTORIA

UGH

Worst thing ever

Will explain later

GABRIELLE

R u ok

VICTORIA

Yeah can't talk

CECILY

K who is meeting me and walking home?

Freezing 🥶 ❄️ ⛄

PRIANKA

Me

Coming

GABRIELLE

Same

Mara, Cecily

M   C

MARA

OMG, Cece

Are u back yet

CECILY

Hi

Yes

Just got back from sledding

I need to thaw out lol

MARA

Did you see what happened

Wayyyyy glad I stayed home

CECILY

Ummm

IDKWYM

MARA

So Mae & Marisa went sledding

I stayed home

Duh

Anyway

Marisa flipped her sled over and into this snowbank ditch FACE-FIRST

And the front of her snow pants totally ripped open!

Jared video'd it & posted and zillions of people have seen it already

He used hashtag #MaRIPa

CECILY

WHAT 😦 😦 ⁉️⁉️⁉️⁉️‼️

CECILY

Like she died?!?!?

MARA

NOOOOO

Because of her ripped pants !!!

CECILY

Ohhhhhh

I knew he was recording all the stuff
but I didn't hear about Marisa

I just got home

That's ridic

How is she doing

MARA

CRYING nonstop

Miserable

MARA

Her mom already left a message for Mr. C

CECILY

OMG

I feel so bad

I didn't see it happen

And obv I'm not on social media

Blargh

MARA

Anyway

Wanted to tell u

CECILY

K

MARA

Did Vic say anything to you about it

CECILY

Umm no

Not yet anyway

MARA

I think her mom saw it on social media
before anyone else

CECILY

What really?????

MARA

Yeah

So nutty

Mae said Vic's mom came to pick
her up right away

CECILY

Wow

I know she got picked up early
but I didn't know why

OMG

I gotta go warm up, tho

Too cold to text

MARA

Bye

Call me later

Victoria, Mom

V   M

MOM

Victoria, get down here this instant

Now

MOM

You must understand that when I see these texts and the horrible sledding posts come up on your social media feeds, I must act. It is my job to keep you safe.

I do not read your texts all the time, but when you're off on your own, I have to stay informed on what you are doing.

VICTORIA

NO YOU DON'T

You don't trust me

MOM

I do not trust the other kids

VICTORIA

You made a whole scene at sledding

I am sooooooo embarrassed

I refuse to talk to you

Vishal, Prianka

V   P

VISHAL

Pri!!!!!

I KNOW I JUST SAW YOU BUT I AM SO
PUMPED 4 U

PRIANKA

Pls stop typing in all caps

But thank you

VISHAL

You're so talented

PRIANKA

LOL I am!!!!

VISHAL

Hahahahahahahah

Can I take you out to celebrate

PRIANKA

Is this real or a joke?

VISHAL

Real!

PRIANKA

Ok, prob not in the snow, tho

VISHAL

LOL I know

Let's go to Jennie's!!!

Do you know they have burrata stuffed with burrata now?

PRIANKA

Really

😲 😲

VISHAL

Yes!

PRIANKA

K I'm in

VISHAL

PRIANKA

VISHAL

Oh wait

PRIANKA

??

VISHAL

Did u see what happened @ sledding
w/ Victoria and her mom

PRIANKA

IDKWYM

VISHAL

She got picked up early after the whole
#MaRIPa thing

I missed this completely

What is #MaRIPa

Brb fone dying

Need to charge it

BFFs

P C V G

PRIANKA

Guys anyone there ??

My fone has been dead for like 2 hours

It wouldn't charge

Need to tell you 2 big things 😨

33

PRIANKA

Also want to check in on Vic 🤍🤍🤍

GABRIELLE

Hi

Just got back from walking my
neighbor's dog 🐶

AGAIN 😫 😫

I asked my mom why she can't help and
she says some responsibility is good for me

😑 😑 😑

PRIANKA

Lol sounds like a mom

GABRIELLE

Vic r u ok??

🤫 🤫 🤫

CECILY

Hi 👋 👋

VICTORIA

I am fine

Thank u for the s'mores kit, Cece
💜 💜 💕 💗 🤍 💝

GABRIELLE

Yeah! Thanks! 🤍 🤍

PRIANKA

Ditto! 🤍

VICTORIA

What are the 2 big things, Pri? 🤔 🤔 🤔

PRIANKA

Wellllllllll

First of allllllll

....

GABRIELLE

Spill it, Pri! 😤 😠 😡

PRIANKA

K

I came in 3rd place in the national teen poetry competition!

There's an awards ceremony & everything!

Maybe u can all come

Think it may be in Fla, though!

Maybe surprise Disney trip!

VICTORIA

Oooohhh

PRIANKA

Soooo that's one fab thing

GABRIELLE

GO, PRI

CECILY

Soooooo awesome, Pri!

PRIANKA

And the other thing...

Vishal kind of asked me out like on
a real date 😲

CECILY

What????

PRIANKA

He wants to take me to Jennie's 🍕 🍕 🍕
to celebrate the win

GABRIELLE

Omg soooooo cute 😍 😍 😍 😍

Can't believe u like him again

After all the women's day stuff
LOL 😆 🤣 😆

PRIANKA

Well yeah

But I taught him the error of his ways
😠 😠 😠

PRIANKA

Such a dummy not understanding the importance of women's day

GABRIELLE

True

VICTORIA

Has V Day dance been scheduled yet

GABRIELLE

I think so yea

But with a community service element

That's the new key to everything @ school

CECILY

Planning meeting soon

VICTORIA

So Pri may have a real date for it?!?!

PRIANKA

Maybe but don't go loony tunes, Vic, LOL
😆 🤣 😆 😝

VICTORIA

Stop

GABRIELLE

What about u and Arjun, Vic? 🤭 🤭 🤭

VICTORIA

IDK we don't talk so much lately 🙍 🙍

Plus I doubt I will be able to go

CECILY

Oh

Really?

VICTORIA

Ugh yeah 😕 😟 😕

Tomorrow after school everyone
come to my 🏠

My mom isn't really letting me out of the house for a while but she said I can have friends over @ my place

Let's all hang in person

Want to talk to all of you & have a 🤍 to 🤍

Can't talk freely over text

CECILY

Ok I'm free ✅

GABRIELLE

Same ✅ ✔

Unless I have to walk the dog again LOL 😆 😂

PRIANKA

Hahahahahahaha 😂 😂

K see u all then

PRIANKA

Going to write more poetry 💔 💔

GABRIELLE

So psyched for you & your win, Pri
🐰 🎉 🥂 🍸

CECILY

ME TOO

Mwah 😘 😘

VICTORIA

YEA, PRI 🍸 🍷 🎉 🎊 ‼️ 💯 💖

GABRIELLE

Xoxo 😘 😘

Gabrielle, Ivy

G   I

GABRIELLE

Hiiiiiii 👋 👋

How's the snow day

IVY

Fun 👏 👏

Yours

GABRIELLE

Fun except blahhhhh I keep having to walk my neighbor's 🐶

& Pri won a poetry contest

I feel like I stink @ everything 😫 😫

IVY

Gabsssss 😪 🙀

IVY

You need to [STOP] [STOP]

You're so hard on yourself 🙅 🙅 🙅

You're an amazing person & friend & ILY
💯 💝 💝 💯 💟 🎈

GABRIELLE

I am I know 😩 🐱

But wahhhhh 😔 😔 😔 😟

IVY

K go chill 🧖

Snow day & everything ⛄ ❄️ ⛄

No sadness 😗 😗

GABRIELLE

Ugh ok

43

How do I find my passion	🔍

Top interests for middle schoolers
What am I good at
How do I find out what I'm good at
Quiz to find out what you're good at
Personality quiz to discover passions
#MaRIPa

Cecily, Mara

C M

CECILY

Hi

Feel so bad for Marisa

MARA

Yeah

She feels sooo embarrassed

MARA

I feel bad for Vic, too

Her mom just totally screamed @ everyone
and like dragged her away

CECILY

Can't believe I was there and missed
all the #MaRIPa drama

MARA

Yeah that's really weird

No offense

Also don't type that

CECILY

OK

I had an idea, though

MARA

What?

CECILY

It just came to me

Out of the blue

What if I got a social media presence but
used it as a force for good

MARA

Force for good LOL

CECILY

For real, tho

Wanted to ask u before I
ask my other friends

We can all be our best selves
so parents don't need to spy

#MaRIPa inspired it

My mom spies, too

Sorry I typed it again

CECILY

Does your mom spy?

MARA

Duh

All moms do

This is a smart idea

CECILY

So you like?

MARA

Yeah!

CECILY

K gonna use this snow day to see if I can
be allowed to have an account

Discuss with the mother etc

MARA

K good luck

MARA

Stay warm

CECILY

You too

POSITIVE VIBES

(V) (G) (C) (P)

VICTORIA

Good morning, friends ☀️ ☀️ ☀️

So excited you're all coming over today 💚 💚

Helloooooooo 👏 👏 ☀️

Where are youuuuuu ❓❓❓❓

See u at school

48

MORE POSITIVE VIBES

CECILY

K guys hi

So glad we're all together rn

Serious talk, tho, so please no emojis

Can't get distracted

PRIANKA

Um 😝 😝 lol ok

Also hi

CECILY

Let's text or whisper so we don't freak out
Mama Melford @ all

Also I brought a new special notebook

CECILY

You know how I am with notebooks lol and this one is gonna be a little diff

We'll only use it for super secret stuff that we're a little scared to say out loud

Wish I'd thought of this when I told u guys I like girls but whatevs

PRIANKA

Such a good idea, Cece

CECILY

Thx

CECILY

Vic, are u ok with it

VICTORIA

Yesssss but nervous to have it in writing

Always nervous about snooping from the moms 😬

Well my mom I guess

GABRIELLE

Same

VICTORIA

Do all of your moms snoop on stuff 🙄 🙄

Be honest

GABRIELLE

Mine def does

CECILY

So does mine

PRIANKA

Duh Mama Basak snoops allllll the time

VICTORIA

That's a little bit of a relief 😌

GABRIELLE

Kinda love this notebook idea & that we can all confess secrets in one place

We will be super careful guarding this one

CECILY

We are always careful duh

GABRIELLE

K true

CECILY

Let's get started

VICTORIA

I know you guys heard by now from people...

But does everyone at school know my mom saw that post & that's why she picked me up early ??

The people who were there when she picked me up from sledding obv know...

GABRIELLE

I don't fully know what happened

Bits and pieces here and there

Can you explain, Vic?

Ok so...

THIS IS SO EMBARRASSING but 😬 😬 😬

She started yelling and lecturing everyone about social cruelty and saying how they should all be ashamed of themselves 😬 😬

But Jared wasn't even there!!

PRIANKA

Ummm

Confused

VICTORIA

Did you all hear all of this or no

CECILY

Not all of it

GABRIELLE

TBH people are more focused on
Marisa I think

She's the one who should be sooooo
embarrassed

I mean hello

#MaRIPa

So don't worry too much about everyone
talking about you and your mom

Ok

Little relief

I delete every text thread as quickly as I can so my mom can't see it but she usually only snoops on my comp when I'm not home and I'm home now so... hopefully safe

CECILY

K

Stop texting now, tho

Notebook time

GABRIELLE

Lol

OK, since I bought the notebook I'm starting this off. This is our safest space ever. Where we can confess our innermost thoughts, share everything we want to without saying it out loud.

Now and forever your friend and truest confidant, Cecily Anderson

Please sign at the bottom of your entry—a contract of sorts that we are all true to one another and safeguarders of each other's secrets.

!!!  STOP !!!

Also: IF YOU ARE NOT CECILY, PRIANKA, GABRIELLE, or VICTORIA, YOU DEFINITELY SHOULD NOT BE READING THIS. STOP NOW!!!!

Cecily Anderson

OK, I'm starting. I'm sorry I didn't tell you right away that my mom saw that post and made a whole scene when she picked me up early from sledding. I was soooooooo embarrassed and sort of thought it would just go away. I couldn't even talk about it.

Yeah, she snoops on social media when I forget to log out of my accounts on my computer. She reads my texts on my computer when I'm not home. I try to delete all threads but they don't always delete. It's so confusing! She's sooooo overprotective and it's a huge issue. And I want it to stop.

Sooooooooooo . . . I've been thinking about it a lot and here's why I think she's so overprotective. THIS IS TOP TOP SECRET. NEVER TELL ANYONE.

When I was four, I begged her to go swimming one day. She kept saying later, later, later. We had to go to the mall to help my dad find suits because he was starting a new job. Anyway, all I wanted to do was swim, so I wandered off at the mall, my parents had no idea . . . I took off my clothes (except undies, duh) and went swimming in the mall fountain.

She was so panicked that I was lost and then when they found me she was SOOOO mortified. Obviously. And it ended up in the local newspaper, on the internet, etc.

Headline: Care for a swim?
DO NOT GOOGLE IT. (PLEASE, PLEASE, PLEASE DO NOT GOOGLE IT.)

Also, soooooo scared my mom won't let me go to the Valentine's Day dance after all of this, and because she gets freaked when there's any possibility of dates or mischief or ANYTHING AT ALL. I mean, she's not even letting me go to people's houses right now.
HELP ME!!!!!!!!

Victoria Melford

Ummmmmm. Wow, that is a lot to take in. I do not know how to respond yet. You were so mischievous, Vic! I love you. I am here for you!!!!

Gabrielle Katz

Wow, Vic. Way too much to write by hand right now. Can we please move this to be a talking thing? Now that it's out in the open. Do you want to leave here and go to my tree house? So private. Haven't been up there in a while & feeling nostalgic. Ooh! Poem alert!

Prianka Basak

Oh, good idea, Pri! Let's do that!!!! OK, Vic? Will your mom let you leave? I love you!!!! HERE FOR YOU FOREVER. DUH.

Cecily Anderson

I'm not really allowed but maybe. I can beg her and say it's for a science project. Let me go check. Xoxo

Victoria Melford

THE SQUAD

V C P G

VICTORIA

So that was a no 😫 😫

She doesn't want me going out right now 😩

CECILY

Ok

PRIANKA

It's cold anyway for tree house ⛄

We'd have to really bundle

GABRIELLE

So so so sorry you're dealing with this, Vic

Are we still going no emojis?

PRIANKA

LOL

CECILY

Can we whisper-talk in person now?

Tired of texting

VICTORIA

Me too

Prianka, Sage

P   S

SAGE

Hi, Pri, my love!

PRIANKA!

Hi 💜 💜

SAGE

Just wanted to say congrats again
🍾 🥂 🍾 🥂

SAGE

Proud of you

PRIANKA

Awwwww thank you my poetry BFF

SAGE

Mwahhhhhhhhhh

VALENTINE'S DAY IS COMING UP

Attention, students! The Valentine's Day dance is
coming up very soon and it will be better than ever!
Planning meeting Friday after school.
Come and share your ideas!
See you there!

Hearts for all!

THE SQUAD

GABRIELLE

Omg u guys

I just had the best idea

U know how the dance needs to have some kind of community service element

What do u think about doing something with St. Francis

PRIANKA

??

GABRIELLE

Bc it's the heart hospital ya know

Get it, hearts? Valentine's Day?

GABRIELLE

Ohhhh and my neighbor was there for her heart surgery

Just remembered

My dog-owning neighbor! 🐶

CECILY

Omg, Gabs
🐧🐧🐧🐧🐧🐧🐧🐧🐧🐧🐧🐧

Such a good idea 💯💯💯💯💯💯

That's where my 🐩 had her open-heart surgery

VICTORIA

Ooh

Sorry just catching up

CECILY

Bring it up at the planning meeting, Gabs
👏👏

GABRIELLE

But I don't really have any more ideas
🤔 🤔 🤔

Like how it would connect

It just came to me

CECILY

K well give it some thought

GABRIELLE

Lol k

Hiiiiii!!!! So I'm still on this quest to find my passion and so far it's not going great. I feel like I need to DO something big. Like all along I've just been coasting and now I really want to do something. The problem is, I can't really come up with any ideas. Plus I feel like I suck. I don't really have much confidence. It's like I want to do something but I also kind of want someone to just do it for me. Ughhhh... grrrrrr. Why am I even telling you this? You're a journal. You can't help me.

Xoxox Gabs

PS Sorry that was rude

Sometimes I want to go sit in my tree house
It would be easy to do
Right in my backyard
My dad even built steps up the tree
I don't, though
Not sure why
I always think about it
But I never go
I think something happens and you realize
You can't go back
To something that once was
Another time
Another phase
Even though the place is still there
Going back just doesn't seem right
In one way it would be so easy
But in all the other ways it's impossible

Prianka the Magnificent

Vishal, Prianka

VISHAL

Yo

Are u involved in this Valentine's Day dance at all

PRIANKA

Not yet

I may go to planning meeting

Why

VISHAL

Just curious

Are peeps bringing dates

PRIANKA

Lol

PRIANKA

How would I know

VISHAL

Hahaha

No clue

U know this stuff

PRIANKA

Not really but thank you 😊 😊

VISHAL

Jennie's this weekend?

BURRATA STUFFED WITH BURRATA

PRIANKA

Kk I'm in

VISHAL

Awesome

Meet there Saturday @ 6 pm

Kk

VISHAL

Jared is in soooo much trouble from #MaRIPa

Suspended for a week

PRIANKA

Whoa

VISHAL

I know

He's dumb

Peace

PRIANKA

Peace

How do you know if you are on a first date 🔍

Best first dates

Worst first dates

How young is too young for dating

Does the person need to pick you up for it
to be a date?

#MaRlPa

Victoria Melford

Melford PA

girl in fountain Melford

Priscilla Melford

Melford Fountain

Vishal
This boy
One day I like him
Then I get nervous
Maybe I don't like him
I think this is normal
But maybe it's not

I was told not to google
I did it anyway
I feel bad
Not telling a soul
Confession done

Prianka the Magnificent

THE SQUAD

G P C V

PRIANKA

Guysssssssss 🖐 🖐 🖐

Vishal & I are really going to Jennie's this weekend

OMG 😳 😲 😳

Helllooooooooooo

Cecily, Mom

C M

CECILY

Hi, Mom

CECILY

I wondered if you've given any more
thought to my social media request

Hello????

MOM

Hi

CECILY

I want you all to trust us and stop
snooping on us

All the moms snoop

MOM

Heading back from grocery store. We can
discuss when I get home. See you soon.
Love you

CECILY

OK

Love you too 💕 💞 💗

THE SQUAD FOREVER

GABRIELLE

Guysssssssss 😫 😫

I am sooo not motivated to do any work

This time of year is sooo blahhhh 😔 😒 😣

CECILY

I feel you

But we have Valentine's Day to look forward to 💕 🐾 🤍 🤍 🥀 🥀 🤍

PRIANKA

Oh

Guess what 😯

Vishal asked about dates for the dance when we talked about Jennie's plans 😯 😯 😯 😯 😯 😯 😯 😯 😯

VICTORIA

WDYM ??

PRIANKA

Like if people are bringing dates

I was like how would I know lol
😆 🤣 😆 😬

CECILY

Omg he totally wants to go with you
!💜!!!💜!!

VICTORIA

Agree 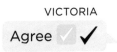 ✔

GABRIELLE

Yessss 💯 💯 💯

ALSO CECE IS DONE WITH EMOJI
HIATUS?!

CECILY

LOL

PRIANKA

Chill guys 😧 😧 😧

You guys never responded to my news

Vishal and I are going to Jennie's THIS
WEEKEND 🍕 🍕 🍕 🍕

CECILY

OMG

How did we miss this?

GABRIELLE

DOUBLE OMG

VICTORIA

That's fab, Pri 🎊 🎀 🎊 🎀

Here's my plan

PRIANKA

Plan for what?

VICTORIA

To get myself to the dance 🐧 💜 🐧 💜

I'm gonna do so much work for the dance there's no way my mom can say no

My neighbor owns a party company and I'm gonna see if she can donate cool stuff

Photo booth maybe?

OH OH OH

They also have all these arcade games

Remember, Gabs, when u mentioned St. Francis?

GABRIELLE

Yeah

VICTORIA

IT CAN BE A FUNDRAISER FOR ST. FRANCIS

OMG I AM ON FIRE

CECILY

LOL go Vic

GABRIELLE

Yeahhhhhh

But I gotta get back to hw 😕 😣 😢

CECILY

Same

VICTORIA

Ugghhhh bye 👋 👋 😘 😘

JK thx for the support ❗️❤️‼️💯

Deleting text thread obvs 👊 👊 💪

Prianka, Sage

PRIANKA

Heyyyyyy 👋 👋

SAGE

Hey 🍷 🍸

PRIANKA

I have a question for u

SAGE

K

PRIANKA

Do u ever think people like to keep secrets to get attention and then trickle out info little by little 🤭 🤭

SAGE

Even your texts sound poetic lol
😆 😆 😆 😆

PRIANKA

Lol!

SAGE

Ummmmm

Kinda yeah ✅

Sometimes people will do whatever it takes to get attention 💀 🤡 🧗 🤸 🤾 🏋️ 🚀 📢

PRIANKA

Yeah agree ✔️

SAGE

Why do u ask

PRIANKA

IDK just curious

SAGE

Yeah right 😕 😕 😕

Tell me

PRIANKA

Promise promise you won't tell anyone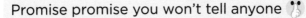

SAGE

Ummmm

Yes promise

PRIANKA

K so if you google Victoria
Melford Philadelphia...

SAGE

Yeah

PRIANKA

Just do it

SAGE

Umm ok hold

Don't see anything yet

PRIANKA

Keep scrolling down

SAGE

Whoa

Reading now

Victoria in her undies in the fountain!?! 😯

As a little kid?? 😰 😰

Who does that?? 😂 😂

I mean even @ 4 it's weird no?

PRIANKA

Hahaha yeah kinda IDK

SAGE

Why do you know this

PRIANKA

She just told us

But it's like this deep dark secret for her

I kinda think it's funny though

SAGE

Yeah it is funny

Anyway I won't tell anyone

PRIANKA

K you BETTER NEVER

SAGE

Sheeesh ok

Anyway did u hear the poetry club may all come to your award reception

PRIANKA

Really 😮 😮

SAGE

Yeah

I overheard Mrs. Marburn talking about it

PRIANKA

Good eavesdropping skills, Sagey
‼️💯‼️💯

SAGE

Lol thanks

I have to confess something 🫣 😔

Speaking of secrets LOL 🤣 🤣

PRIANKA

Yeah ⁇

SAGE

I was soooo jealous of your win at first
😢 😢 😢

But I want you to know I am happy
for you 👏 👏

PRIANKA

Oh, Sage 😔 😿 😔 😿

Thank you for telling me

And being open and honest

SAGE

Xoxoxo

SAGE

Is Vic ok though for real ❓❓

Not the fountain thing but after the whole scene w/ her mom @ sledding yelling @ everyone

PRIANKA

U know about it, too ❓❓❓❓❓❓

SAGE

Umm yeah

Everyone does

PRIANKA

Ohhhh 😤 😠 😡

She's ok

She doesn't think the whole grade knows

Let's keep it that way 🥷 👍 👍

Another secret I guess... 🙌 🙌

Kk

Xoxoxoxo

Gabby,
Thanks so much for walking
Elroy my wonder pup! He
loves you! I wonder if you are
interested in keeping this up.
Maybe a little part-time job.
Let me know. No pressure if
it's too much.
Thank you!
Xoxo
You neighbor,
Mrs. Minkin

<u>Ideas to make Valentine's Day more meaningful:</u>

• Make heart artwork for people at Yorkville Nursing Home

• Visit cardiac patients at St. Francis

• Make little care packages of sweets for kids who visit the soup kitchen

• Have a raffle and donate money to refugee families in Yorkville

• Have photos all around the gym of different kinds of couples

• Show love for all people

• Take all phones away during the dance to focus on being in the moment

• Make each student write a pledge to become more considerate & loving

• Have a Post-it wall of goals to become more loving

• Have a Post-it wall of things we love

Have members of dance committee present ideas & plans @ next PTA meeting to parents

Dear Mara,
I don't want to
just want you to

be too overwhelming but
know my feelings for
still very much there.

you are true and
See you soon,
Cecily

WOO!!!!!

GABRIELLE

Guys!

I am soooo fired up 🐧🐧🐧🐧

GABRIELLE

That planning meeting was awesome
👏 👏 👏 👏

Everyone seemed into the St. Francis
idea and I think it can really work
💗 💗 💗 💗 💗 💗

We can make cards for the patients and
then go to drop off 🌏 💜 💟 💔 💚

Was it bad not to mention fundraiser idea?

Didn't want to steal Vic's thunder

PRIANKA

Yeah good idea to wait on that

CECILY

Love it, Gabs 🤍 🤍 🤍

LOL sorry for the pun 😆 🤣 😆

PRIANKA

Hahahahahahahahah 😆 😆 😆 😆 😆

PRIANKA

Love day every day! 😑 😑 😑 😑

GABRIELLE

Ooooh that can be the theme
of the dance 💝 ‼️ 💯

PRIANKA

Yesssssssss 💯

Vic where r u now

GABRIELLE

She left school early

PRIANKA

Oh no

CECILY

So sad she missed the planning meeting
😔 😕 ☹️ 🥺

But so pumped we can present @ next
PTA meeting

CECILY

Getting the parents excited will be key

Especially Mama Melford

GABRIELLE

Vicccccc

Where rrrrr uuuuuuu ??????

PRIANKA

K stop harassing her

CECILY

Gabs do u feel like you're closer to finding your passion 🤔 🤔 🤔

GABRIELLE

Not really 😕 ☹️

PRIANKA

What else can you do??

GABRIELLE

Now u r harassing me 😫 😖 🤔 👻

GABRIELLE

But I'm gonna be rich 💵 💲 💵 🤑 💰

PRIANKA

??

GABRIELLE

Gonna be walking the neighbor's 🐶 Elroy more often & get 💲 for it

CECILY

Wooooo 👏 👏 👏 👏

PRIANKA

Wow that's great 🎎 🎇 🎎 🧜

GABRIELLE

Thanx 😆 😆

TTYL

CECILY

Mwah

PRIANKA

😗 😗 😗 😗

BFFs

G C P V

GABRIELLE

Oh one more thing ‼️

Did u hear they're letting people from
other schools come to the dance

Maybe Ivy will want to join

She could sleep over after

CECILY

Oooh really

Fun 🩴 🩴

PRIANKA

That's a cool idea

GABRIELLE

People need to sign something,
though, and get a reference from
their own school 😖 😖 😖

GABRIELLE

Like for safety

How nutty is that 😲 😲

PRIANKA

Omg wow ❗❗❗

What kind of reference 🤤

GABRIELLE

From like a teacher or something 🙍 🙍

CECILY

Omg

I wonder if anyone wants to come that
badly to go through that 🙁 🙁 🙁

PRIANKA

Lol, Cece, but I get what
you're saying 🤣 😆

CECILY

Like it'll be fun but that fun?? 🙍 🙍

GABRIELLE

🤣 🤣

IDK

Guess we'll see

Gabrielle, Miriam

MIRIAM

Omg Sami might come for the
V Day dance 😩 😩

GABRIELLE

Really 😯 😯

Is she allowed ⁉️ ⁉️ ⁉️

MIRIAM

Well yeah they're allowing out
of school people

I know but she literally got kicked out of school soooo... 😆

Haha true

Did you hear Eloise is bringing her boyfriend from her theater group

No omg 🙀 🙀

Didn't know that they were so serious ‼️‼️‼️‼️

Oh yeah ❗💜

They are 💜💜

She tried to sneak out of her house once to go see him 🙀 🙀

He lives around the corner but still

GABRIELLE

Lol wow 🙈 🙈 🙈

MIRIAM

I kinda wanna bring this boy
Jonah from camp

He's soooo cute 😍 😍 😍 😍

GABRIELLE

Send me a pic

MIRIAM

K hold

GABRIELLE

Ooooh he's cute 💯 💯

MIRIAM

I feel nervous asking him, tho

GABRIELLE

Does he live far away

MIRIAM

Not really

GABRIELLE

Hmmmm

Just make it seem like a low-key thing

MIRIAM

IDK

I'll think about it 😅 😅 😅

GABRIELLE

K good luck

Can't believe we'll see Sami again

MIRIAM

LOL I see her all the time

GABRIELLE

I know

I mean the rest of us

MIRIAM

It'll be fun

She's chilled out a bit

GABRIELLE

She has 😛 😛 😛

MIRIAM

Pretty much yeah

GABRIELLE

K cool

Gotta go walk neighbor 🐶 Elroy

He's cute

GABRIELLE

MIRIAM

Xoxoxo

SQUAD FOREVER

G V P C

GABRIELLE

hiiiiiiii

Guys guess what

VICTORIA

What ????????

Sorry I have been so MIA

My mom has been picking me up
right after school 😿 😿 😿 😿 😿

102

And I have been trying to stay off text so she'd chill on snooping

Don't think it's working

Anyway...what?

GABRIELLE

I'm gonna be going to my first wedding 👰 🤵 💐 🏰

Ya know how I have one cousin on my dad's side but he's way older and we never see him and I barely know him

PRIANKA

Ummm sounds kinda familiar but IDK

GABRIELLE

Anyway so he's getting married 🤵 🤵

In 2 months 😺 😺 😺

And my dad & I are going
👯 💃 👯 👯 💃 👯

CECILY

So fun

PRIANKA

Can we go 👗 shopping with you

Is it a major fancy wedding

GABRIELLE

IDK

Yeah my dad texted me a pic of the invite

Says black tie ❗💍❗❗

VICTORIA

Oooohhhhhh

Too bad ur too old to be
a flower girl 😲 ☹️ 😥

GABRIELLE

Yeah that would be awk 😆 😆

CECILY

This is gonna be so fun, Gabs ❗❗❗❗❗

104

GABRIELLE

IK ‼️

I'm excited 🐤🐤🐤🐤🐤🐤🐤

VICTORIA

R u gonna have to dance
with ur dad 😛 😛 ☹️ ☹️ ☹️

GABRIELLE

Umm maybe

PRIANKA

Is that awk ❓❓

GABRIELLE

Not really

He's pretty low key

PRIANKA

So cool 💯

I've only been to 1 wedding and it
was a hardcore Indian wedding
so this will be way diff 🎎 💃

GABRIELLE

Yeah Jewish weddings are
kinda hardcore, too ☑ ☑ ✔

Lots of specific traditions

Plus a super long dance called the hora

You know it from bar and bat mitzvahs

They raise the bride and groom
in chairs and everyone dances
around them 👰 🤵 💃 💃 💃

My mom has a book on Jewish weddings
and I skimmed it once when I was bored
so I know about allllll the traditions now
LOL 😄 🤣 😄

PRIANKA

Wow ❗❗❗

U must've been really bored 🤣 🤣 🤣

CECILY

LOL, PRI!!!

PRIANKA

Sorry true tho 😊 😊

GABRIELLE

Yeah I was reallllllllyyyyyyyy
bored LOL 🤸 🤸

So yeah all these rituals and stuff
that I don't understand

CECILY

So fun, tho 🧜 🧜 🧜 🧜

GABRIELLE

K back to hw for me 🙌 🙌 🙌 🙌

CECILY

Same

Good luck w/ everything, Vic

VICTORIA

Thx

PRIANKA

Ta ta loves 😘 😘

From: Gabrielle Katz
To: Doug Katz
Subject: Wedding

Hi, Dad!

I am sooooooo excited about cousin Ethan's wedding. I know we haven't seen him in so long but I've never been to a wedding! YAY! Thanks for texting me a pic of the invitation. It's so pretty. We're gonna have so much fun!

Xoxox Gabs

Gabrielle, Prianka

G   P

GABRIELLE

Omg I can't even believe this
😲 😞 😐 🙁 😢

GABRIELLE

Wedding is same weekend as the awards
reception for the poetry contest

PRIANKA

OMG WHAT 😮

GABRIELLE

I just checked the calendar

PRIANKA

Oh nooooooooo 😕 ☹️ 😕 ☹️

GABRIELLE

I am sooo sad 😕 😕

I can't do both ☹️ 😿

PRIANKA

Me too 😩 😿 😩 😿

GABRIELLE

What am I gonna do

PRIANKA

Ack IDK

PRIANKA

I can video reception for you

GABRIELLE

But all of our friends are going & I hate to miss group stuff 😟 😟 😟 😟

Will feel so left out 😩 😩 😩 😩

PRIANKA

But u are sooo excited for wedding 💍 ‼️ 💍 ‼️

Plus you see us alllll the time

GABRIELLE

I know but still

Wahhhhh 😩 😩 😩 😩 😩 😩

Why does stuff like this have to happen 😩 😩 😩 😩 😩 😩

PRIANKA

IDK

PRIANKA

So annoying

GABRIELLE

Grrrrr

Grumpy again

PRIANKA

Sorry, Gabs 😞 😞

We'll fig something out

Gotta go to bal vihar

GABRIELLE

K have fun learning about your heritage 😎

Love u

PRIANKA

Love u

BFFS

V G P C

VICTORIA

hiiiiiiii

Are all ur moms @ the Parents in Action meeting rn

Why do parents have so many meetings anyway

Super stressed

GABRIELLE

😲 😲 😲 😲 😲

VICTORIA

Can we make this a non-emoji conv

Really feeling anxious

PRIANKA

Wow that is big for you to not want emojis

PRIANKA

Ummm IDK if my mom is there

I'm just getting home from bal vihar

Carpooling with Arj...

VICTORIA

LOL

PRIANKA

Why do u ask

VICTORIA

My mom is at the meeting rn & I'm
nervous the dance is gonna come up

CECILY

My mom is @ the meeting, too

GABRIELLE

Mine, too

Don't stress, Vic

GABRIELLE

The dance is totally PG

VICTORIA

IK but my mom always goes bonkers

PRIANKA

Hahaha, Vic

U gotta chill

U can't control her

VICTORIA

Um duh but she can control me and not let me go and get dance canceled maybe

Who knows what she can do

CECILY

Parents in Action is different, tho

I don't think they talk about the dance and plans there

PRIANKA

Chill

VICTORIA

K gtg

CECILY

It's gonna be ok

Sending 🤍 🤍 🤍

To: Mr. Carransey
From: Victoria Melford
Subject: Valentine's Day Dance

Dear Mr. C:

I know we are trying to bring more of a community service element to the dance and so I have an amazing idea! I missed the planning meeting the other day but I will definitely be at the next one.

We should make it a fundraiser for St. Francis Hospital (THE HEART HOSPITAL). I know we're already doing stuff with them but if we make it a fundraiser, it would be great.

My neighbor owns Party Like It's 1999 party company and they are willing to donate a photo booth, three arcade games, and some centerpieces if it's a fundraiser.

What do you think?

Thanks for considering!

Victoria Melford

sent from my iPad

quick side chat

C G P

CECILY

Guys

No side chats but

Quick side chat & don't hate because of it

Also sticking w/ non emojis for a bit, too

I think we need to be more sensitive
to Vic & her issues with her mom

They seem difficult

GABRIELLE

Yeah

PRIANKA

I don't get it, tho

What is the actual thing going on

117

CECILY

Hard to say

PRIANKA

I know the fountain thing when she was
little but can that still be so so hard for her?

CECILY

IDK

It's like her mom can't deal with
her growing up AT ALL

All our moms snoop but
Mama Melford is different

And really gets intense

GABRIELLE

Hmmm

CECILY

I'm just saying we need to be more aware

PRIANKA

Ur prob right, Cece

PRIANKA

How are u always so in touch w/ people

Ur like a psychic therapist mastermind
genius or something

CECILY

LOL that is a lot of things, Pri

PRIANKA

So true, tho

CECILY

IDK I just get a sense that Vic
really struggles with it even though
she doesn't talk about it much

GABRIELLE

Yeah

Maybe she'll wanna talk about it one day

CECILY

K this side chat is getting too gossipy

PRIANKA

Love how you started it, Cece, and now you're putting the kibosh

GABRIELLE

Lol kibosh

Such a funny word

PRIANKA

Wanna know another word I love

CECILY

Ya

PRIANKA

Lackluster

Isn't that a good one

CECILY

So good

I love words

PRIANKA

Me too duh

GABRIELLE

K guys this has been fun

PRIANKA

I gotta get ready for Jennie's w/ Vishal

GABRIELLE

Oooh have fun

LOVE YA

PRIANKA

Thanks! Mwah 💋 💋

CECILY

Mwah mwah mwah

HAVE SO MUCH FUN

SQUAD 4 Life

V G C P

U guyssssss 👏 👏

Since I had to leave early and I missed the dance planning meeting the other day, I emailed Mr. C about how I think it should be a fundraiser for St. Francis

GABRIELLE

OMGGGGGGG sooo glad you wrote him 💯 💯 💯 💯

Vic that is 🤓 🏆

VICTORIA

And party company will donate stuff 🎗 🎎 🏴‍☠️ ✴️ ❇️ 👏

CECILY

Yessssss 👏 👏 👏 👏 👏 👏

CECILY

Love how you're so pumped up, Vic

VICTORIA

Yaaayyyyyyy ‼️🏆❣️‼️

To: Victoria Melford
From: Edward Carransey
Subject: RE: Valentine's Day Dance

Dear Victoria,

What an incredible idea! I am thrilled you're taking initiative with the dance! We can most certainly make it a fundraiser for St. Francis. Let's discuss in more depth next week.

Thank you very much,
Mr. C

sent from my iPhone. Please excuse typos

Gabrielle, Mom

GABRIELLE

Hi, Mom 👐 😗 😗

MOM

Hi 💕

Why are we texting when we are sitting on the same couch? 😊 😊

GABRIELLE

It's fun 😊 😊 😊 😊 😊 😊 😊 😊 😊 😊

MOM

Ok

Hi

GABRIELLE

Can u take me shopping for a dress for Ethan's wedding 💃 💃

GABRIELLE

I know I just got new dresses
for bat mitzvahs

But please 🤤 🤤 🤤 🖤 🖤

MOM

Let me think about it

Maybe we will split and you will
use half of your dog walking $

GABRIELLE

That could be good

Also

Can we look into me volunteering at YAS

MOM

YAS?

GABRIELLE

Yorkville Animal Shelter

MOM

Oh!

Sure!

GABRIELLE

Could be great for me right?

MOM

Definitely

Love to see you taking an
interest in something

GABRIELLE

Such a mom comment

MOM

I am a mom LOL LOL

GABRIELLE

Hahahahah

Ok coming to snuggle

MOM

😘 😘 😘 😘

SQUAD 4 Life

(V) (G) (C) (P)

PRIANKA

You guysssssss 🤚 🤚 🤚

Jennie's w/ Vishal was soooo much fun 🍕 🍕 😀 😀 👯 👯

CECILY

Yayyyyyyy that is soo sooooo great

GABRIELLE

PRI!!!! 💕 🤍 🤍 💖 💘 💖

127

GABRIELLE

First date!!!! 💝 💘 🤍 🍼 😘

VICTORIA

WOOOO

Deleting this text chain

BRB

No talk of dates for Mama Melford
to snoop on 🐩 🐩 🐩 🐩 🐩

PRIANKA

K

Done

From: Gabrielle Katz
To: Yorkville Animal Shelter
Subject: volunteering

Dear Yorkville Animal Shelter:

I wanted to find out about volunteer programs for middle school kids. I love dogs and I want to help. Please get back to me.

Thank you,
Gabrielle Katz

Victoria, Mom

V M

VICTORIA

Mom

I am begging you

Please don't go nuts about
the Valentine's Day dance

Normal for kids to take dates
& it's totally innocent

And it's not like everyone is taking dates

I mean most kids are not

I am begging you

MOM

Victoria, I will do what I think is right

MOM

This is not your concern

VICTORIA

It is my concern

It's a FUNDRAISER for ST. FRANCIS

And Edward is donating all this
stuff from the party company

I thought of asking him all on my own

I really took initiative

I really care about this

I'm really involved in the dance

Please listen to me

Please let me go

MOM

Victoria. Stop.

I feel like what happened when I was 4 @ the mall has spooked you for life and now you can't function like a normal person

You can never face it

And it is ruining your life

And my life, too

MOM

Enough

Get your coat

Time for school

SQUAD 4 Life

V G C P

VICTORIA

Guys !!!!

I need to call an emergency meeting 😨 😨 🦮 🤮

Not at my house, tho

Where can we meet after school SOS SOS SOS SOS SOS SOS

My mom is letting me go to friends' houses again

FINALLY THANK THE LORD

Get back to me asap please 🙏🙏🙏🙏🙏🙏

Need to use special secret shared notebook 📓 📓 🧕 🙈

Let's call it SSSNB

Where r u guyssssss 😤 😤 😴 😴 ✖️ 😴

From: Cecily Anderson
To: Gabrielle Katz, Victoria Melford, Prianka Basak
Subject: Today

Hi! Vic, I saw the texts but couldn't respond so I'm moving this to email and hopefully you all check in study hall today. Don't want to bring up at lunch in case it's super emotional and private.

Anyway, do you want to come over to my house? We can meet after school. My mom has a meeting and Ingrid has lacrosse tryouts.

Write back or just show up! Or drop me a locker note to say you're coming!

Xoxox Cece

See you after school! No time to email.
Xo Pri

I'm coming over! Woo! So much to discuss.
Xoxoxoxoxoxoxoxox GABS!

Thanks for having us over. Love, Vic

Hi guys, thanks for all meeting at Cece's. I'm really having serious issues with some stuff and I haven't been open about it and I wonder if there are things going on with you, too, that you haven't been open about. I think we can all be honest about this. I don't want to make this a Struggle Journal but maybe it will turn into that. I've been realizing that I suffer alone a lot of the time but I don't want to. I want to lean on others and get help. So that's why I called this emergency meeting. I want to write about my problems and then I hope you guys respond and then you can write about yours maybe and then we can all be honest and rely on one another. Sound OK? OK!

I am freaking out over things with my mom. She seems to want to derail all things and keep me locked up like a baby. I'm such a good person, rule follower, get good grades, all of that. And yet she barely wants me to go out, and she's already freaking out over the Valentine's Day Dance even with all of my hard work. I mean, I'm getting a free photo booth and ARCADE GAMES! HOW AWESOME IS THAT? And what if I can't even enjoy it?!?

I think deep down she is always afraid!!! That's why she yelled at everyone at sledding and made such a scene. IT WAS THE WORST.

Why is my mom like this??? Why can't she be like your moms???

I don't know what to do. I just really, really want to take some action. I feel like I am missing my whole life.

Passing to Cece now. Love, Vic

First of all, Vic, I think this is super brave of you. We do need to lean on each other and you have a lot going on in your head and it's not healthy to keep it all in. I struggle with feeling the need to be perfect. You guys all know that. And also the whole thing about liking girls and not being totally sure where to go with it. It just feels like I'm alone in that and it's something that will get easier with time. I'm not really sure.

But enough about me.

Vic, I wonder if you could ever talk to your dad about this stuff. Have you tried? I know it can be awkward with dads but maybe it can work? And if not, I wonder if the school psychologist or your guidance counselor can help. Sometimes it helps to get other people involved. Just a few ideas. Passing to Gabs. LOVE YOU ALL FOREVER AND EVER,

Cece

Hi! OK, so you know my main stuff so I won't bore you with that again. Obv the ADHD thing and my school frustrations and all of that. But also it's more. I want to find my passion and I have been working on that and I may have found it but stay tuned and also enough about me. I think that we need to try and get your mom to be more social with our moms. I think it'll really help. Can we plan a brunch or dinner or something very soon? Before the dance? And then all the moms can talk to your mom and maybe help her relax a little? Great idea, right??? Passing to Pri. Xoxo Gabs

Hiiiiiii, LOVIES!!! Well obvs I have no worries at all because I'm Prianka Basak the extraordinary and a poetry champion so yeah. HAHAHAHAHAHAHAHA!!! JK! Of course I have problems. DUH. WE ALL DO. Which is why I'm obsessed with this journal and putting it all out there, maybe in poetry form. HAHA. JK again! See, I am trying to bring the humor here!

OK, anyway. I love Gabs's idea and I think we need to do it right away. I love that you're reaching out to us, Vic, and love that we can all be honest about our stuff and I love our friendship and I LOVE ALL OF YOU SOOOOO MUCH! SMOOCHES FOREVER, Pri

Hi! So what if my mom sends an email to everyone?
Mama Anderson is good @ organizing.

Wait!!! We can't let my mom know that we are
sort of forcing it on her. We need to make it
seem like a normal plan somehow that she drops
me off at, and then maybe they encourage her to
stay? I don't know. She doesn't like forced things.
UGH SHE DOESN'T SEEM TO LIKE ANYTHING.
WAHHHHH.

Good point, Vic. We don't want her to feel awk
and then not even come.

Agree. Maybe we all get ready for the dance
together and the moms come? But if you're not
allowed to go to the dance that won't work.

Maybe we can all go out for ice cream together after a PTA meeting when we are presenting since we know Mama Melford goes to those!

Genius!! We won't plan it. Just pray it happens after PTA meeting.

Cecily, Mom

C M

Mom?

Are you there

MOM

Hi

Yes

Downstairs

CECILY

Can we text

MOM

Um, sure. Why, though?

CECILY

Don't want Dad to weigh
in and make jokes

143

MOM

Ok

CECILY

Can you help me with Vic's mom?

MOM

What's going on?

I'd really prefer to discuss this face-to-face

CECILY

MOMMMMMMMM

MOM

OK, come down and discuss, please

CECILY

Fine

Bye

From: Yorkville Animal Shelter
To: Gabrielle Katz
Subject: RE: volunteering

Hello, Ms. Katz!

We'd be thrilled to have you volunteer. Normally our volunteers are 18+ but we have had a great deal of interest from middle schoolers and so we are starting a middle school volunteer program. It meets on Saturdays from 3-5 and it can fulfill school community service requirements, although we are not saying you are doing it for that reason. :)
Please let us know when you would like to begin. You can email back, call, or stop by the shelter.

Puppy love!
Marren Fleetis
Director, Yorkville Animal Shelter

> **From:** Gabrielle Katz
> **To:** Yorkville Animal Shelter
> **Subject:** volunteering

Dear Yorkville Animal Shelter:

I wanted to find out about volunteer programs for middle school kids. I love dogs and I want to help. Please get back to me.

Thank you,
Gabrielle Katz

SQUAD 4 Life

V G C P

GABRIELLE

Guys ❗❗❗❗

Guess what 🐧🐧

Yorkville Animal Shelter has a middle school kids volunteer program on Saturdays & I'm gonna do it! Anyone wanna do it with me 🐾 🐶🐶🐶

PASSION ALERT 💯💯💯💯

I think I wanna be a vet when I grow up 🐶🐱🐶🐩🐭🐹🐸🐵🐥🦆🐝🦋

CECILY

Wooo 💯 so awesome, Gabs

GABRIELLE

Feeling pumped 👊👊👊👊👊

CECILY

WOOOOO TO ALL ‼️💘❗💘‼️💯

PRIANKA

New life motto 💯

"Woo to all!"

CECILY

Love it 😍😍😍😍😍😍

K bye 👏👏

GABRIELLE

Mwah 😘😘

PRIANKA

Mwah 😘😘

From: Cecily Anderson
To: Edward Carransey
Subject: New Initiative

Dear Mr. Carransey,

I stopped by your office earlier but you were in a meeting. I want to start something new. I had to check with my mom first, though.

It's called SOCIAL MEDIA FOR GOOD AND NOT FOR EVIL. Everyone will sign a pledge that they vow to use social media in a different way. It won't be for leaving people out or bullying someone or anything like that. The situation with the viral video of Marisa (#MaRIPa) was horrible. I know Jared got in trouble and was suspended for a week but we need to really take it a step further.

It seems like it all started with the whole thing with Sami and the ranking and the #broboom thing and now the video. Social media has become toxic to the extreme. I really want to make this change. Please let me know what you think.

Thank you, Cecily Anderson

I am not afraid of storms, for I am learning how to sail my ship.
—Louisa May Alcott

Dear Journal,

I realized something. I only turn to you when I'm upset and that's not fair. Maybe it's because I take the good stuff for granted and I don't write it down. Or maybe it's because the bad stuff always feels more important. But anyway, I need to turn to you when I feel good, too. And guess what? Today I feel good! I think I've finally found my passion: animals! Dogs, specifically. And I get to volunteer at the Yorkville Animal Shelter on Saturdays. It's gonna be great. Plus my friends and I are really all getting along right now and we're trying to help Victoria with her issues with her mom. I feel like I need to pause and appreciate this moment. Thank you for all of your support. ;)
Xoxo Gabs

MY LOVES

V C G P

VICTORIA

GUYSSSSSSS 😵 😲 ✗✗ 😮

OMG 😨 😨 😨 😨 😨 😨 😨 😨 😨 😨

I know it is late but Cece, my mom just got off the phone with your mom and they talked for an hour!!!!!!!!!!!!!!!!

👏 👏 👊 👊 👊

I didn't even know she was calling!!

CECILY

OMG 👊 👊 👊 👊 👊 👊 👊 👊 👊 👊 👊 👊 👊 👊 👊

I didn't know for sure either but they talk sometimes at PTA meetings sooo...

I was eavesdropping, too
😆 🤣 😂 😆 🤣 😆

VICTORIA

Since we are going to the PTA meeting
to talk about the dance my mom said
OK to ice cream after

CECILY

THIS IS HUGE, VIC

VICTORIA

I KNOW

SOOOOO excited

GABRIELLE

Wait!!! When is this happening??

CECILY

Monday

GABRIELLE

Oh, I forgot dance committee is going
to PTA meeting to discuss plans

PRIANKA

This is community service, too, LOL
😂 🤣 😂 😂 🤣 😂

GABRIELLE
❗❗❗❗❗❗▪❗❗

CECILY

K great 💯

VICTORIA

U GUYS 💝❗❗💝❗❗💝❗❗

I am soooo excited my mom agreed
🎎 🎉 🎎 👯 👯

PRIANKA

WOO TO ALL
👏 👏 👏 👏 👏 👏

CECILY

WOO TO ALL
💯 💯 💯 💯 💯 💯 💯 💯

GABRIELLE

WOO TO ALL

VICTORIA

LOL WOO TO ALL

From: Cecily Anderson
To: Prianka Basak, Gabrielle Katz, Victoria Melford
Subject: MISSION FOR ICE CREAM DATE

Hi, guys!

Sorry for all caps in subject line but I am just soooooo excited and can't keep chill in study hall!!!!
OK, so goals:
Get Vic's mom to chill out re: dance and date and all other kids growing up stuff
Get moms to stop snooping (prob not gonna accomplish this in one night but worth a try!)
HANG OUT & HAVE SO MUCH FUN
EAT ICE CREAM!!!!!!!!!!!!!!!!!!!!!!!!!!!!!!!!!!!!
I AM SOOOOOOO EXCITED.

xoxoxoxoxoxoxoxoxoxoxxo Cece

From: Edward Carransey
To: Cecily Anderson
Subject: RE: New Initiative

Dear Cecily,

So sorry for my delay in responding. I LOVE this idea. Also, thrilled the dance committee will be at the PTA meeting on Monday. Stop by my office on Monday morning to discuss further.
Wonderful thinking!

Mr. Carransey

sent from my iPhone. Please excuse typos

> **From:** Cecily Anderson
> **To:** Edward Carransey
> **Subject:** New Initiative
>
> Dear Mr. Carransey,
>
> I stopped by your office earlier but you were in a meeting. I want to start

something new. I had to check with my mom first, though.

It's called SOCIAL MEDIA FOR GOOD AND NOT FOR EVIL. Everyone will sign a pledge that they vow to use social media in a different way. It won't be for leaving people out or bullying someone or anything like that. The situation with the viral video of Marisa (#MaRIPa) was horrible. I know Jared got in trouble and was suspended for a week but we need to really take it a step further.

It seems like it all started with the whole thing with Sami and the ranking and the #broboom thing and now the video. Social media has become toxic to the extreme. I really want to make this change. Please let me know what you think.

Thank you, Cecily Anderson

I am not afraid of storms, for I am learning how to sail my ship.
—Louisa May Alcott

THE CREW 4life

G C P V

GABRIELLE

Hiiii guyssssss 👋👋👋👋👋👋

How amazing was that meeting?

Side note...

Maybe I should start a dog-sitting business? 🤔🤔🤔

CECILY

Ooh

Meeting was so fab ✅✔️✅✔️

PRIANKA

YAYYYYYYYY 🎊

AGREE

PRIANKA

Vic, all the parents
LOOOOVEEEEEDDDDDD
the fundraiser idea 🙌 🙌

VICTORIA

OMG ‼️

CECILY

Also the moms are totally chatting
& bonding rn 🌷 🌷 🌷 🌷 🌷

Soooooo excited
☂️ 🧜 ☂️ 🧜 🧜 ☂️ 🧜 ☂️ 🧜 🧜

VICTORIA

Let's eavesdrop & feel out the vibe for
Mama Melford & the dance 👀 👀 🌷 🧜

CECILY

Feel out the vibe is our new
group motto ‼️ 🌷

GABRIELLE

LOL 😆 🤸

GABRIELLE

U love mottos, Cece

CECILY

I DO ❗🎈‼️

Social media for good and not for evil

Woo to all

Feel out the vibe

I think that's it

WOO TO ALL

🙂 🙂 🙃 🙂 🙃

Stop texting for a bit and eat

THE CREW 4life

G C P V

GABRIELLE

K who has the best hearing
out of all of us 🤭 🤭 🤭

PRIANKA

I've been eavesdropping
this whole time 🙍 🙍 🙍

They're explaining to Vic's mom how chill
our town is compared to others ☮ ☮ ☮

Cece, ur mom is talking about Ingrid and
how she didn't grow up too fast and how
everything is age appropriate ❗🍭‼

CECILY

That's kinda true 🍭 🍭 🍭

VICTORIA

What is my mom saying 🙍 🙍

162

PRIANKA

She's saying she trusts you but doesn't
trust others 😦 😦 😦

VICTORIA

LOL that's always her go to
😒 😒 😒 😒 😒 😒 😒 😒 😒 😒 😒 😒

PRIANKA

So she feels like you should skip the dance
bc it may get wild 😦 🥺 😦 🥺 😦 🥺

My mom is zoned out 👩‍💬 😶

I think she feels its ok since she knows I
love Vishal lol 🤭 🤭 🤭 🩶 🩶 😆 🤣 😆 😆

CECILY

She knows that?? 😆 😆 😆

PRIANKA

Yes duh

All the moms in the Indian community
want us to get married hahahahahah
😆 🤣 😆 🤣 😆 🤣

PRIANKA

Vic did your mom know u loved
Arjun for a time 😂 😂 😂 😂

VICTORIA

No wayyyyyyyyyyyy

GABRIELLE

Why did that even fizzle

Also do the moms think it's weird we're
not even talking and just sitting here next
to each other texting & eating

PRIANKA

They don't seem to notice...or care LOL

VICTORIA

It fizzled bc I got bored of it

GABRIELLE

Got it

Ok

PRIANKA

Anyway

I think they'll make progress
with your mom, tho, Vic

VICTORIA

You do??

PRIANKA

Yeah 👏 👏

Gotta be patient and wait this out

VICTORIA

She doesn't like people to
tell her what to do, tho

PRIANKA

They're def not

Just chatting

Seems chill

VICTORIA

VICTORIA

I just want to have a normal mom

Literally all I've ever wanted

CECILY

But haven't we talked about this?

How no one is normal

VICTORIA

Lol yeah

But like your moms

I just want her to be like that

GABRIELLE

Kk

They snoop, though, too

We told u that

It's different

GABRIELLE

IKWYM

PRIANKA

Wait omg

Vic, your mom just confessed something

VICTORIA

????

PRIANKA

About the incident at the mall

How she's never dealt with it

How she's always afraid all the time

It consumes her she said

Mama Basak just had great idea

PRIANKA

She said your mom should write you a
letter and open up about her feelings

VICTORIA

Really?

Wowwww

I can't even believe she
is opening up to them

GABRIELLE

Our moms are kinda magic

The original baby yoga crew LOL

But happy to welcome Mama Melford in

VICTORIA

😖 😖 😖 😖 😖 😖 😖 😖 😖 😖 😖 😖 😖

So choked up

CECILY

Same

But let's stop texting

Let's lighten this up a bit

Can we play this game
Ingrid told me about

So much fun

GABRIELLE

Yessssss 🔪. 🎢 🧜 🧜

CECILY

Should we include the moms???

VICTORIA

Ummmmm

GABRIELLE

Good for bonding

Let's do it

GABRIELLE

Can't believe they're letting us stay
out so late on a school night

Let's see how long this lasts...

I LOVE YOU GUYS

GABRIELLE

OMGGGGG !!!!!!

Who knew our moms could be so funny
😂🤣😂🤣

This game is sooo much fun

CECILY

Srsly

CECILY

I am most likely to organize a protest
🤭 🤭 🤭

PRIANKA

UMMMM

At least you're not most likely to fall
asleep eating a burrito 😆 🤣 😆 😆

VICTORIA

OMG thought my mom was gonna
flip when she got most likely to ask to
speak to the manager 😆 😆 😆 😆

LOL

GABRIELLE

Honestly this is so funny

My mom is most likely to offer to
host the super bowl party and not
show up hahahahahahahahahah

GABRIELLE

This is the bestttttttt gameeeeeee 😂 😂

VICTORIA

This is the first time I've heard my mom laugh in foreverrrrrrr 🙌🙌🙌🙌

I want to always remember
To take a step back
To appreciate
And admire the magic of friendship
It is a gift
We realize it again and again and again
These people fill me up
They see me
They understand me
They accept me
Sisters
Real-life sisters
Even though we're
Not
Even
Related

Vishal, Prianka

V P

VISHAL

Yo

PRIANKA

Yo

VISHAL

Still thinking about our Jennie's visit

PRIANKA

Yeah

VISHAL

But I have to confess something

TBH I think that might have been too much burrata

PRIANKA

LOL

PRIANKA

Kind of agree

VISHAL

You're cool, Pri

PRIANKA

Right back atcha

Gonna go to bed now

VISHAL

Later, Pri

PRIANKA

Later

VISHAL

Sweet dreams

FRIENDSSSSSSSSSSSSSSSSS

P C G V

PRIANKA

Anyone up??????

I know it's so late

But I can't sleep

And Vishal just texted

And I looooove him

CECILY

Hi!

I'm up, too

Too wired to sleep

PRIANKA

Right??

CECILY

Ya so happy how ice cream date went

PRIANKA

Me toooooo

Dear Victoria,

Prianka's mother gave me this idea to write you a note and it feels funny but I am going to try it. I prefer face-to-face, but maybe this will be easier for me to express my thoughts.

You are right that I am overprotective. It has always been hard for me. To be honest, motherhood is challenging. You are my precious gem and I worry all the time that something will happen to you. I know you can't understand but perhaps you will when you're a mother yourself. If you want to be.

The incident at the mall when you were four completely scarred me for life. You were missing for twenty minutes. It felt like an eternity. Beyond that, you could have drowned in the fountain. I always felt like it was my fault. I didn't keep you safe.

But I got a second chance and somehow the universe saved us. But what if that was a one-time thing? I always fear that I will lose you, my most precious treasure. I always feel like I will fail at keeping you safe.

I am going to try and be more relaxed. I know you have done so much with the dance. I am proud of you and I don't want to hold you back from going. It scares me that students from other schools will attend. I don't know if I can trust anyone. I have trouble with that.

I am glad I can be open with you and I hope we will forge a new path of understanding.

I love you more than words can ever express.

Mom

FRIENDSSSSSSSSSSSSSSSS

VICTORIA

Um guys

This may be bad form

But I am taking a pic of the letter my mom wrote me and sending to you

Hellloooo

Ok here it is

Keep this top top top secret

Hi guys

I am regretting that I sent that

Please delete immediately

CECILY

K

GABRIELLE

K

PRIANKA

K

Dear Mom,

I don't even know what to say.
Thank you for opening up to
me and for being honest.
I love you so much,
Victoria

PS Does this mean I can go to
the dance?

OMG, Vic—now that a few days have passed, how do you feel? BTW, adding initials at the ends of our entries in case we read this decades later and we forget who wrote what. OK? We need this to be accurate. —PB

I feel really relieved. I think we are on a new path and it's a good one. —VM

Sooooo poetic!!!! —PB

I agree!!!!! Such a good first step! And we have so much fab stuff coming up!!!!! –GK

I know—this is really such a huge year. —PB

Woo to all! –GK

Woo to all!!!! —PB

Woo to all!!!!!! —VM

Woo to all FOREVER. —CA

Vic, does this mean you can go to the dance???
—PB

I think so!!!!! —VM

BEST FRIENDS FOREVER

V C P G

VICTORIA

Can everyone come to my house to get ready for the dance?

Obv my mom wants to take tons of pics

She said she can drive us all over, too

PRIANKA

Fine with me

Just soooooo excited

CECILY

Yayyyyyyyyyyyy

GABRIELLE

Works for me, toooooooooo

185

BEST FRIENDS FOREVER

V C P G

VICTORIA

Just want to take one minute before we leave for the dance to say how grateful I am for you guys and all of your help with everything. I know we are all together but we can't talk freely in front of moms, duh, and I just love you all so so so much.

Only one thing left to say...

Woo to all

Woo to all x2

Woo to all x3

Woo to all x4

GLOSSARY

2 to

2gether together

2morrow tomorrow

4 for

4eva forever

4get forget

any1 anyone

awk awkward

bc because

BFF best friends forever

BFFAE best friends forever and ever

BI Block Island

BNF best neighbors forever

b-room bathroom

b/t between

c see

caf cafeteria

comm committee

COMO crying over missing out

comp computer

deets details

def definitely

DEK don't even know

diff different

disc discussion

emo emotional

every1 everyone

fab fabulous

fabolicious extra fabulous

fac faculty

fave favorite

Fla Florida

FOMO fear of missing out

fone phone

FYI for your information

gd god

gg gotta go

gma grandma

gn good night

gnight good night

gr8 great

gtg got to go

hw homework

ICB I can't believe

IDC I don't care

IDEK I don't even know

IDK I don't know

IHNC I have no clue

IK I know

IKWYM I know what you mean

ILY I love you

ILYSM I love you so much

JK just kidding

K OK

KIA know-it-all

KWIM know what I mean

l8r later

LMK let me know

LOL laugh out loud

luv love

n e way anyway

NM nothing much

nums numbers

nvm never mind

obv obviously

obvi obviously

obvs obviously

OMG oh my God

ooc out of control

PBFF poetry best friend forever

peeps people

perf perfect

pgs pages

plzzzz please

pos possibly

q question

r are/our

ridic ridiculous

rlly really

RN right now

sci science

sec second

sem semester

scheds schedules

shud should

some1 someone

SWAK sealed with a kiss

TBH to be honest

thx thanks

tm tomorrow

TMI too much information

tmrw tomorrow

tomrw tomorrow

tomw tomorrow

totes totally

ttyl talk to you later

u you

ur your; you're

urself yourself

vv very, very

w/ with

wb write back

whatev whatever

WIGO what is going on

wknd weekend

w/o without

WTH what the heck

wud would

wut what

wuzzzz what's

Y why

ACKNOWLEDGMENTS

Many, many thanks to: Dave, Aleah, Hazel, the Greenwalds, the Rosenbergs, my BWL Library & Tech crew, Alyssa Eisner Henkin, Maria Barbo and the whole Harper Collins/Katherine Tegen crew: Katherine Tegen, Jon Howard, Gweneth Morton, Sara Schonfeld, Molly Fehr, Amy Ryan, Kristen Eckhardt, Vaishali Nayak, Sam Benson, and Jessica White. Last but never least: my ultimate gratitude to all of the readers!

Photo by Peter Dressel

LISA GREENWALD lives in NYC 🍎 w/ her husband & 2 young daughters 👨👩👧👧. She 🤍s: 😎 📚 🖊 & 📚. Summer is her favorite season ☀️ 🌞 🍉 🍒 🍦 🎁 🕶. Visit her 💻 @ www.lisagreenwald.com.

If you like TBH, you'll love this other series by Lisa Greenwald!

Start reading on the next page!

ONE

"KAYLAN!" RYAN POUNDS ON MY door. "You overslept! School starts today! You're already late!"

I run to beat him over the head with my pillow, but I'm too slow. "Ryan," I shout down the hall. "You're a jerk! Karma's a thing, you know. Bad things will happen to you if you're not nice to me."

After five deep breaths, I call Ari.

"You want to go to the pool?" I ask her as soon as she answers.

She replies in her sleepy voice, "Kay, look at the clock."

I flip over onto my side, and glance toward my night table. 8:37.

"Okay," I reply. "I'll admit: I thought it was later. At least nine." I pause a second. "Sorry. Did I wake you?"

Ari sighs. "I'm still in bed, but you didn't wake me."

"Agita Day," I tell her. "August first, red-alert agita levels. I'm freaking out over here."

August 1 signals the end of summer, even though you still have almost a month left. August 1 means school is starting really soon, even though it's still twenty-nine days away.

"Oh, Kaylan." She laughs. "Take a few deep breaths. I'll get my bathing suit on and be at your house in an hour. I already have my pool bag packed because I had a feeling you'd be stressing."

"Perfect." I sigh with relief. "Come as soon as possible! But definitely by nine thirty-seven, okay? You said an hour."

"Okay. I'm up. And you're never going to believe this," she says, half distracted. "I'm getting new across-the-street neighbors."

"Really?" I finally get out of bed and grab my purple one-piece from my dresser drawer. "Describe."

She pauses a second, and I'm not totally sure she heard me. "They're moving the couch in right now," she explains. "I can't tell how many kids there are, but there's one who looks like he's our age."

"A boy?" I squeal.

"Yeah, he's playing basketball right now." She stops talking. "Oops, he just hit one of the movers in the head with the ball."

"Tell me more," I say, dabbing sunscreen dots all over my face. They say it takes at least a half hour for it to really absorb into the skin, and my fair Irish complexion needs all the pro-tection it can get.

I only take after my Italian ancestors in the agita depart-ment, I guess.

"He went inside," she explains. "I think he got in trouble. I saw a woman, probably his mom, shaking her hands at him."

"Oops." I step into my bathing suit, holding the phone in the crook of my neck.

"Oh wait, now they're back outside. Taking a family photo in front of the house." She pauses. "He has a little sister. I think they're biracial. White mom. Black dad."

"Interesting," I say. "Maybe his sister is Gemma's age!"

"Maybe . . ." I can tell she's still staring out the window at them, only half listening to me.

"By the way, Ryan is insisting that red X thing is true. You haven't heard about that, right?" I ask.

"Kaylan!" she snaps in a jokey way. "No! He's totally mess-ing with you. Okay, go get your pool bag ready, eat breakfast, and I'll be there as soon as I can."

I grab my backpack and throw in my sunscreen, a change of clothes, and the summer reading book I haven't finished yet. I'm having a hard time getting into *My Brother Sam Is Dead*, although from what I've read, it makes my life seem pretty easy.

I hear Ari's instructions in my head as I get ready, and I

already feel calmer. Her soft voice—she's never really flustered by anything.

I stare at my watch again. 9:35. I wait for Ari on the front steps. I'm trying to stay as far away from my brother as possible. Ari still has two minutes, but I wish she was here already.

I stand up and look for her, but she's nowhere in sight. She is so going to be late. On Agita Day.

I learned the word *agita* from my mom. She's part Italian and she learned it from her grandmother, who was 100 percent Italian and apparently said it all the time. It basically means anxiety, stress, heartburn, aggravation—stuff like that.

I don't know what my great-grandma's agita was about, but mine is pretty clear.

Starting middle school.

A few minutes later, I spot Ari at the end of the block, and I walk down the driveway to meet her. She strolls toward me, hair up in a bun, with her favorite heart sunglasses on. Her pink-and-white-striped tote hangs over her shoulder like it's the lightest thing in the world.

"I brought you an extra hair tie," she says, showing me her wrist. "Since you always forget."

"Thanks," I say. "Let's go in so I can grab my stuff. I've had the worst morning."